Daddy,
Do Cowboys
Pray?

JAMES R. EZELL, JR.

FIRST EDITION

ISBN: 978-1-936989-55-3

Library of Congress Control Number: 2012916405

Published by
NewBookPublishing.com, a division of Reliance Media, Inc.
2395 Apopka Blvd., #200, Apopka, FL 32703
NewBookPublishing.com

Printed in the United States of America

Introduction

Pray? Why pray? What can praying do? Many children and adults ask the same question.

Faithful parents are always concerned as their children grow to having more role models than just their parents. We know that other influences that surround them are not always the ones we would want for them.

Join Zeke as he asks the same question, "Why pray? Who prays? What can praying do?" Explore these questions with Zeke as he begins to understand that not everyone prays, including his friends and heroes. And, like so many people, he is looking for answers.

As a parent who has been blessed with the title "Daddy" by my adopted, biological and foster children, I have a deep desire to help them, and everyone with whom I come in contact, to develop a better understanding of the world we live in and gently guide them to make the most important decision of their life. While not everyone believes the Gospel message of Jesus Christ, it is the choice of every individual to make this decision. As much as we would like to be able to make this decision for them, the only thing we can ultimately do is guide them to explore these answers for themselves. I was inspired by the Holy Spirit to write "Daddy, Do Cowboys Pray?" for that reason.

The Bible is filled with stories of the faithful and unfaithful, and their trials and victories. Follow Zeke as he finds heroes, and villains, along *his* journey as well.

You will be inspired, and you will laugh and be held in suspense as the story unfolds. As he comes of age, Zeke understands that not everyone prays, and he wonders about the necessity of prayer. He questions whether or not his tough-guy, hero types like cowboys pray. His father suggests a plan to find the answer. So they take a road trip to a real working ranch where Zeke gets a few surprises, and learns some lessons as well.

As they make the journey, he encounters a few "other" heroes along the way and learns something about their prayer life...what they pray, why they pray, where they pray, when they pray, and sometimes, amazingly, who they pray for.

So join Zeke and explore the question so many people are asking today. Who knows? You may find the answer you are looking for, as well.

Chapter 1

"**Z**eke! Zeke! Come here…look!" Jeff Buffington shouted over to his son.

Zeke stopped playing ball. "What is it, Daddy?" he yelled as he ran over.

"It's a rainbow," his dad said, pointing to the sky. "Look! Have you ever seen one as bright as that before?"

"Wow, it's beautiful!" Zeke said, wide-eyed. "Where did it come from?"

Jeff was always looking for ways to teach his son about God. "God made it just for us. It's to remind us that He loves us very much."

"Wow! That's awesome! He did that for *me*?"

"He did, indeed. What do you think *we* should do?"

Zeke looked puzzled. Then he said slowly, "Thank Him?"

"Yes, I think that's a fine idea. How do you plan to thank Him?" his dad asked, smiling.

"Maybe, um…when I pray tonight," the boy said, smiling back.

As happens in many families, his parents had taught Zeke to pray early. They wanted him to grow up knowing about God and how He loves us more than anything.

Zeke had quickly learned his bedtime prayer and said it nightly. "Now I lay me down to sleep, I pray the Lord my soul to keep. Send angels to watch me through the night, and keep me safe till morning light. Amen."

Sometimes, he would hurry through his mealtime prayer. That way, he could start eating more quickly. "God is great. God is good. Let us thank Him for our food. Amen," he would say quickly.

Now, he and his dad sat admiring the rainbow. Zeke was looking into the distance. He began to think about the new prayer he would be praying. It made him feel different. He would not be praying a memorized prayer, but a more personal prayer.

After sitting for a few minutes, Zeke looked up. "Dad, is it true that not everybody prays?" he asked.

His dad's smile faded. Then he said sadly, "It is true. Not everyone prays. But many people who love God and are happy that he loves us *do* pray."

Zeke thought about this and about all of his heroes. Then he began asking questions. "Do football players pray? Do teachers pray? Do firemen pray?"

"Many of them do," his dad said.

"What do they pray? Do they thank God for rainbows?"

Zeke paused to catch his breath. Then he turned and looked at his father. "Do cowboys pray?" he asked.

His dad took a deep breath. "I don't know if cowboys pray," he said. "But I do know how we can find out. Would you like to ask a real cowboy that question?"

Chapter 2

Several weeks later, the alarm clock went off at 4:00 in the morning. Zeke's dad got out of bed and went to the kitchen. When he got there, he found Zeke watching the coffee pot drip.

Rubbing his eyes, the boy asked, "Daddy, can I have some coffee, too?"

"Maybe a little in your chocolate milk," his dad said. "You're up early. Are you excited about our trip?"

"Yes, sir. I couldn't sleep. When will we get to the ranch?"

"We'll be there in a couple of days," his dad replied. "We have a few stops to make first. Grandpa is going to be so excited to see you! Now hurry up and get dressed. We have to go to the airport."

Zeke's mom came into the kitchen. "Are you ready for your big trip?" she asked her son. "I filled your backpack with snacks and books."

"Mom, I get to see a real cowboy and Grandpa, too! I wish you were going with us."

"Maybe I can go on the next trip. I know you and your daddy will have a lot of fun. I'll be praying for you while you're gone. Will you pray for me?"

"Um, yes, ma'am. Are you sick?" Zeke asked.

"No, but I'll be missing you," his mom said.

A little bit later, Zeke and his dad were in the car. "Bye, Mom," Zeke said as she shut the door on his side. "I love you!"

"Buckle up, buddy," his dad said, starting the car. "We have a long way to go before we get to the airport."

After a while, Zeke worked up the nerve to say something he had worried about. "Dad, sometimes when I pray at school, some of the kids make fun of me."

"What do they say?" his dad asked.

"Well, Bobby said he doesn't pray and I'm not supposed to pray in school. He laughs at me and asks if I'm praying for the food to taste better. Why can't I pray at school?"

"Zeke, that is a very good question. Many people are confused by something called separation of church and state. Have you heard of that before?"

"I think so. But I don't know what it means."

"Well, it means our country is the greatest in the world because we have freedom of religion. So we can worship as we please. And the government does not tell us how we should worship or who should lead it.

"Taxpayers pay for the schools and the government runs

them. So it is against the law for anyone at the school to lead you in worship. But it is *not* against the law for you to pray in school. You can pray any way or pray any where you like. You can give thanks for your meal. You can pray before a test. You can even pray for your teachers and friends."

"Yeah, but I'll still get picked on and laughed at," Zeke said. "I bet cowboys don't get picked on. I bet they don't pray."

"That's why we are taking this trip," his dad said. "So you can ask one and find out."

Chapter 3

They arrived at the airport and unloaded their suitcases as the sun came up. Then they got on the shuttle bus and rode to the airport terminal.

Zeke's dad pointed to the eastern sky. "Look, Zeke!" he said. Sunlight was coming through the clouds in streaks of yellow, orange, and white. "God sure has a way of saying, 'Good morning,' doesn't He?"

"Wow, that's almost as cool as the big rainbow we saw!" Zeke said. "God sure does paint well!"

When they got to the security check, lots of people were taking their shoes off. Zeke asked his dad why. His dad explained that it was to keep bad guys off the plane. Then he reminded his son about September 11, 2001.

Zeke said, "I remember my teachers telling us about that. It was a bad day. They said some people hate Americans. Is that why Mommy always prays when you leave on a trip?"

"Mommy prays when I leave?" his dad asked.

"Every single time you walk out the door," Zeke replied.

"I like to hear that," his dad said. "Oh, look, Zeke. Isn't that your teacher, Miss Betty?"

Zeke waved. "Miss Betty! Miss Betty!" he called. "What are you doing here? Guess what? I'm going to see a real cowboy!"

Miss Betty looked up and smiled. "Zeke, what a surprise!" she said. "So you're going to see a real cowboy?"

"Yes! Dad is taking me to see Grandpa and then to a dude ranch. We're on a journey to find out if cowboys pray. Where are *you* going?"

"I'm going to see my mom in Arizona. She isn't feeling well. So, you want to find out if cowboys pray?"

Miss Betty had taught Zeke in pre-school. He liked her very much. Now, he beamed as he told her about the rainbow. He also told her about Bobby picking on him. And he told her about talking with his dad about who prayed and who didn't.

When he told her his dad said teachers can't lead students in prayer, she nodded. Then she said, "Your dad is right. We are not supposed to lead you in worship. But I do have the freedom to pray for you any time I want to. And I did pray for you every day that I taught you. I prayed for all of the children I taught, and I still do."

"Wow!" Zeke said. "You prayed for me when I was your student?"

"I sure did! Jesus put it in my heart to teach children, and to pray for them. The Bible says in Matthew 19:13-14 that the little children were brought to Jesus. This was so he could place his hands on them and pray."

"I remember that part," Zeke said.

"Good!" Missy Betty said. "That is why I teach, and that is why I pray for you and others. I have to get on my plane now. Will you do me a favor? Will you pray for my mom and me?"

"Yes, I will, Miss Betty," Zeke said.

"Thank you, Zeke," Miss Betty said. "And please let me know what cowboys say about praying."

Chapter 4

Soon, the plane began loading and everyone got in line to show their tickets. As Zeke looked for their seats, he read the numbers out loud. "There's row sixteen and seventeen. Oh, there's eighteen! And there are our seats!"

"Good for you," his dad said.

"Can I sit by the window?" Zeke asked. His dad nodded and he sat down and buckled up. Then he watched the ground crews and other planes take off and land.

As people kept passing by, an older gentleman stopped. He put his bag up and sat down in the seat beside Zeke's dad. "I'm Bart," he said.

Zeke's dad looked at him and said "I'm Jeff and this is Zeke." Then he asked, "Did you use to direct traffic and talk to the kids in front of the junior high school?"

"I sure did," the man said. "It was one of the most rewarding jobs I ever had."

"I remember you! My friends and I knew you were a detective. But you were always directing traffic and talking with the kids."

"I remember someone asked why in the world I was there directing traffic," Bart said, laughing. "He wanted to know why I wasn't out chasing bad guys."

"That was me," Zeke's dad said. "And your answer has stuck with me for over 25 years. You said, 'Son, I just want to help as many kids as I can to get over fool's hill now, so I don't have to chase after them later.'"

Bart smiled and said, "And that's still my goal today." Then he looked at Zeke and asked, "Zeke, is this your first flight? Where are you going?"

Zeke said, "Yes, sir. We are going to see Grandpa. And then we're going to a dude ranch to find out if cowboys pray."

"Cowboys, huh? Those guys are real tough men, aren't they? I've known a few tough guys in my time," Bart said.

"Have you ever shot anybody?" Zeke asked him.

"Thankfully, no, I have not had to shoot anyone," the detective answered. "But I have arrested a bunch of bad guys and a few cowboys, too."

"You arrested cowboys? Did they put up a fight?"

"Well, some of them did. I remember one time we had a real big dude holed up in a little cabin outside of town. I prayed that we could get him out without hurting him, or having him hurt anyone else."

"You prayed for a bad guy?" Zeke asked in surprise.

"I pray every day for the bad guys. Jesus taught us a lot about praying for others. He prayed for those who were crucifying Him, asking God to forgive them. I pray for bad guys, because I think sometimes they don't know there is a better way. I try to teach the Gospel to those I have to arrest. I want them to know God loves them and, with His help, they can move on to a better life."

"Did they pray?" Zeke asked.

"Some prayed and accepted Jesus as their Savior, and went on to live crime-free lives," Bart said.

"The cowboys, I mean," Zeke said. "Did they pray?"

"You know, Zeke, I don't remember if the cowboys I arrested prayed or not. I would like to think they did."

Bart and Zeke's dad started talking about some of the people they knew. Some had made it over what Bart called fool's hill, and some never did. While they talked, Zeke looked out the window at the changing landscape below.

Pretty soon, the plane landed in Kansas City. Zeke and his dad and Bart headed off to the baggage claim area.

Bart grabbed his bag first. Then he asked Zeke, "Will you let me know what you find out about cowboys? I will be praying for you on your journey."

Zeke smiled and nodded. Then he asked Bart, "Will you come to my school and direct traffic one day?"

The detective smiled. "I sure will, Zeke," he said. "Thank you for asking!"

Chapter 5

Zeke and his dad loaded their bags into the rental car. Then Zeke asked, "How long until we get to Grandpa's house?"

"About 20 minutes," his dad said. "Your grandfather is going to be so happy to see you!"

When they pulled into the driveway, Grandpa was waiting on the porch. He opened the car door and gave Zeke a big hug. Then he picked Zeke up and tried to swing him around.

"Hey, he is too big for that. You will hurt your back!" Zeke's dad said, laughing.

"No kidding," Grandpa said, setting him down. "Come on in. I've got a surprise for Zeke."

Grandpa's house was on a golf course. It had a garden and was also near a lake. He loved to play golf and fish and work in the garden. He was also very active in his church. "Idle hands are the devil's workshop," he often told his son.

"Here you go, Zeke. Check this out," Grandpa said. Then he gave the boy a football.

"Cool!" Zeke said. "Why is it white?"

"That's so the autograph will show up better," Grandpa replied.

"What autograph...where?" Zeke asked, and turned the ball around to look.

"The one you're going to get this afternoon," Grandpa said. "The Kansas City Chiefs' quarterback will be at a bookstore autographing his new book. You might get him to sign that."

"All right!" said Zeke.

Chapter 6

After Zeke and his dad settled in, Grandpa showed them around his garden of flowers, tomatoes, and fruit trees. Then he took them for a ride in his golf cart, and they met some of his golfing pals. Grandpa told them all about the journey Zeke was taking to find out if cowboys pray.

After lunch, Zeke's dad took a nap in the recliner. So Zeke and Grandpa went for a boat ride along the lakeshore.

"Grandpa, you sure have a lot of stuff to do," said Zeke. "I like hanging out with you!"

"I like hanging out with you, too," Grandpa said. "I just wish your grandmother was still here. She'd be proud to see how you've grown, and how responsible you are."

"Responsible?" asked Zeke.

"Yes," Grandpa replied. "It takes a very responsible young man to seek answers to questions. Many people don't have answers, and don't try to find them. I think it is very wise for you and your father to go on this trip. Jesus said, 'Seek and you shall find; knock and the door will be opened; and ask and you shall receive.'"

"Why don't some people look for answers, Grandpa?"

"I don't know. Maybe they don't know they need to look. They're kind of like the sheep Jesus says just wander around. They have no clue that a wolf is at the edge of the woods. Some might know they are in danger and need answers, but are afraid of those answers."

"What do you mean, Grandpa?"

"Well, it's kind of like an ostrich, sticking his head in the sand to avoid seeing danger," his grandfather said. "The danger is there, but it makes him feel better not to see it. If he sees it, he has to do something about it. And too many people don't want to change."

"That doesn't sound very smart," Zeke said.

"Like I said, you're very wise for such a young man," Grandpa said with a smile.

Zeke sat silently as they rode back to the dock. He watched the waves and the birds as the boat zoomed past the lakeshore. When they got out of the boat, he asked, "Grandpa, what if I find out that cowboys don't pray?"

"I'm sure you will figure out what to do about it," Grandpa said, patting Zeke on the back. "Now, let's get cleaned up and go to town."

Chapter 7

Carrying the white football, Zeke walked with his dad toward the bookstore. "Are you getting an autographed Brett Jones book?" he asked.

"I sure am!" his dad said. "You know I like books."

"Yeah, but I didn't think you liked books about football."

"Well, you're right," his dad said. "But Brett Jones is a great quarterback *and* a born-again Christian. The book is about how God changed his life."

"So, it's *not* about football?" Zeke asked.

"I'm sure there are some football stories in the book," his dad said. "Playing football is what he does for a living."

"Oh, good," said Zeke. "Will you show those to me?"

"Sure, kiddo. Look, there's Brett at that table! I need to buy a book. And there's Grandpa. See? He's standing next to Brett."

Zeke hurried over to the table where his grandfather was

talking to Brett and the owner of the bookstore. Grandpa was telling them about Zeke's journey to meet a real cowboy and find out if cowboys pray.

While he smiled and signed books, Brett listened to Grandpa. When his turn came, Zeke handed the ball to Brett. "Would you please sign this?" he asked.

"Sure," said Brett. "You're Zeke, right? So, you're going to see some cowboys, huh? I hope they're nicer to you than they were to me. They sacked me five times the last time I went to see them."

"I'm not going to see the *Dallas* Cowboys!" Zeke said, laughing. "I'm going to see real cowboys on a ranch."

"They're even tougher than Dallas…right?" Brett asked. Then he handed the signed football back to Zeke.

"Yes, sir," Zeke said. He turned the ball around and read out loud what Brett had written. "To Zeke, my Friend in Christ! Brett Jones, Job 42:10."

"Wow, thanks, Mr. Jones! My dad is getting one of your books. He said it's about how God changed your life."

"It is, Zeke. I was not very wise in the way I handled success. So I drifted away from God," Brett said. "I grew up in church and learned about God. But I never really accepted the gift of salvation He gave me in Christ. And I didn't really know how to pray.

"I knew all the words, but I didn't know what it meant to really experience God. I made a mess of things and almost lost my wife and kids, because I let football and success become my

God. Then I turned back to God and asked Jesus to come into my heart and be my Lord and Savior.

"After that, I began praying for the other players who did not know Christ. And I also prayed for His help in leading a more peaceful and godly life. My prayers were answered, so I wanted to share those things with others through this book."

"You pray for the other football players?" Zeke asked in surprise.

"I sure do, Zeke. I pray for my teammates *and* my opponents. It's too bad, but there are still a lot of people that do not believe in God. So I pray for them every day," Brett said.

Zeke looked at the crowd that had gathered to hear him talk to Brett. Then he looked down at the floor. "I'll bet they don't make fun of you like Bobby does me," he said quietly.

"Sure, they do," Brett said. "So I just pray even more for them!"

Zeke stuck out his hand and said, "Thank you for the autograph. I'm sorry I didn't cheer for you against Dallas. I will next season."

Brett laughed and the people in the crowd clapped their hands. "Great!" Brett said. "I need all the fans I can get, especially if they will pray for me."

Chapter 8

The next morning Zeke put his autographed football in the car and helped his dad load their bags. Then they hugged Grandpa and headed to the airport.

After checking in and boarding, they settled into their seats for takeoff. Zeke's dad was reading his book. Zeke was spinning his football, and looking at Brett's autograph from time to time.

"What is the Lazy Bar Z Ranch like, Dad?" he asked. "Is it like those old cowboy movies on TV?"

"Let's look at the brochure," his dad replied. "It says here the Lazy Bar Z is a working dude ranch where they raise cattle and horses. We'll be staying in a bunkhouse and eating at the big house with the other guests and the ranch hands.

"We can go horseback riding, hiking, and swimming. And we can ride with the ranch hands to watch them do their chores. We'll camp out under the stars on a trail ride and listen to the cowboys tell stories and sing songs. That will be like those old movies."

"What kind of chores do cowboys do?" Zeke asked.

"It says here that they mend fences, feed the livestock, and round up strays. Think you'd like to help them do those things?"

"Uh, could I maybe just watch?" Zeke asked.

"I'm sure you can," his dad said, laughing.

After they picked up their bags, they saw several drivers holding signs with names on them.

"Are we going to have our own driver?" Zeke asked.

"Yes. Someone will pick us up. In fact, I think I see him," his dad said, pointing.

Zeke turned and saw a scruffy man in faded blue jeans, a denim shirt, and a crumpled black hat. He had a long, scraggly beard and small, round wire-rimmed glasses. He was holding a sign with Zeke's name on it.

Chapter 9

Zeke took a step back, and stared at the man. The man stared back. Then he held the sign towards Zeke and said, "Zis your name?"

"Yes, sir," Zeke said.

"Z'em your bags?" the man asked.

"Yes, sir," Zeke said again.

"M'name's Rooster," the man said. "You lookin' ta go ta the Lazy Bar Z?"

"Yes, we are," Zeke's dad replied.

"You must be Zeke's pappy, Mr. Buffington," the driver said, extending his hand to Jeff. "Glad to meetcha, and you too, Zeke."

"Glad to meet you, Mr. Rooster," Zeke said.

The man laughed. "It's jus' Rooster," he said. "No need ta get all fancy. It's jus' plain Rooster."

Rooster loaded the bags on a cart and wheeled them out to a beat-up, old SUV. A woman got out, introduced herself as

Nancy, and helped Rooster load the bags. After they were seated in the car, she said, "Buckle up. It's a long, bumpy ride."

As they drove, Rooster pointed out landmarks and ranches. He told them he was born and raised in the area, and knew everyone. He pointed out Dry Gulch, a deep and colorful canyon, and told Zeke the largest rattlesnakes he had ever seen lived there.

Rooster knew the name of every ranch along the way. He knew who the owners were, and how many kids, grandkids, and cattle they had. Zeke kept turning his head to see everything.

At one point, he asked Rooster, "Are you a real cowboy?"

Rooster shook his head "Well, I don't do the roundin' up of the cattle with the rest of the hands. And I'm not ridin' the range an' fixin' the fences an' stuff. But I goes along wif 'em and feeds 'em good after they been workin' all day. I'll be feedin' you, too, if you go out wif'em. You aimin' to be a real cowboy, Zeke?"

"I'm not sure," Zeke said. "But I want to talk to them."

Just then, Nancy yelled, "We're here! Welcome to the Lazy Bar Z Ranch. Let's get you boys unloaded and into the bunkhouse, so you can start exploring the place."

As they piled out, she told Rooster to put the bags in their bunkhouse, and then to head over to the kitchen. He had to load the chuck wagon for the ranch hands that were out on the range.

Then she turned to Zeke and his dad. "Glad to have you here," she said. "I'll see you later at the main house. In the meantime, make yourself at home!"

Chapter 10

They followed Rooster to the bunkhouse and quickly unpacked before heading out to explore the ranch. First, they saw a corral with about a dozen horses near the barn. As Zeke climbed up on the rails to look at them, a couple of the horses walked over to visit. Zeke was a little nervous, but he reached out and rubbed their foreheads. Then he said, "They sure are beautiful animals."

"God's creations never cease to amaze me," his dad replied.

"Which one will I get to ride?" Zeke asked.

"I'm sure they will pick one for you that's friendly and easy to handle. Which one do you like?"

"This one seems really nice," Zeke said, rubbing a dark colored Appaloosa with a speckled rump and a white streak on its face. "Do you think I can ride him?"

"That's Blaze," said someone behind them. "That's the

best one in the whole bunch."

Zeke and his dad turned to see a tall man looking every bit like cowboys from an old western movie, complete with chaps, hat, scarf, and vest.

"Hi, I'm Scooter," the man said. "Nancy told me to check on y'all." He shook hands with Zeke's dad, and then reached out to rub the horse's face. "Blaze is one of the smartest horses I've ever trained."

"You train horses?" Zeke asked.

"I sure do," Scooter said. "I work for Mr. Parker who owns the ranch. He asked me to sign on a few years back, because I have a special knack for talking to horses."

"You *talk* to horses?" Zeke asked.

"Well, not really talk to them like you and I talk," said Scooter. "But I understand what they are thinking or feeling by the way they act and move. I use my actions in ways they seem to understand. That's how I train them. Here's what I mean."

Scooter raised his hand and Blaze backed up a few steps. He swung his arms to the right, and Blaze turned. Then he swung his arms to the left, and Blaze turned the other way.

"Wow, that's neat!" said Zeke.

"It is pretty cool," said Scooter. "I wish I could deal with people that easily! Talking to horses and God seems to be easy for me; but talking to people, not so much."

Scooter put his hand out and Blaze came up to him. He hooked a lead rope to the horse's halter and turned to Zeke. "I need to take Blaze over to that pasture over there," he said.

"How about a short ride?"

"Sure!" Zeke said excitedly. As he climbed down from the rail, Scooter picked him up and set him onto Blaze's back. While they walked along, Scooter and Zeke's dad talked.

On Blaze's back, Zeke relaxed and thought about what Scooter said about talking to God. Then he said, "So you must be a real cowboy."

Scooter laughed. "Well, I don't know about that. But I do know a lot about horses. That's why Mr. Parker calls me the Gentle Horseman. But I don't do a lot of the chores the cowboys do. That's a rough and tumble bunch!"

Zeke looked at his dad and asked, "When will we see the cowboys?"

As Scooter opened the gate, he pointed at the barn where Rooster was loading supplies. "Ol' Rooster is going out to the range this evening to cook dinner for a bunch of them," he said. "Maybe you can ride along."

Scooter helped Zeke off Blaze's back. Then he unsnapped the lead rope and let Blaze take off across the pasture, galloping, and kicking.

As they turned to go, Zeke's dad thanked Scooter. Then Zeke asked, "Do you know if the cowboys pray?"

Scooter scratched his chin. "Do cowboys pray? Now that's an interesting question! I'm guessing that's why you wanted to see a cowboy, huh?"

"I reckon," Zeke replied, sounding more like a cowboy by the minute.

Chapter 11

As they approached the barn, Zeke and his dad could hear Rooster talking. They weren't sure if he was talking to the horses, the wagon, or himself. He just seemed to like talking to everything. They asked if they could ride along with him, and eat with the cowboys out on the range.

"Shore can," he said, "But, you'll be a missin' dinner in the big house wif Miz Nancy. It's a long ride out and you'll hafta stay all night."

Jeff looked at his son and said, "It's up to you, buddy."

Zeke nodded. Then he asked Rooster, "Can I hold the reins some on the wagon?"

With all the supplies loaded, they headed out to the range. Rooster talked and talked. He told them all about the guys they were going to see. He said Boots was an old-timer with lots of stories and lots of scars from stringing fence. He said one time a barbed wire he had strung too tight broke and hit him across his face. He told them Rabbit spent every weekend in town partying, and C.B. was new to cowboying.

Zeke asked, "Is that all of them?"

"Nah, thar's ol' Coop. He don't say much, and sticks to hisself mostly. He's one fur real cowboy, tougher'n nails, and likes wrestlin' steers, and shootin' coyotes."

Zeke looked at his dad excitedly. Finally, he was going to meet a real cowboy!

They drove around a bend and saw a whole herd of cattle and a handful of cowboys on horseback. Rooster drove the wagon to a clump of trees, stopped, then hopped out. Zeke and his dad climbed down to watch the cowboys moving the cattle, whistling, calling, and cutting them into position.

The first cowboy to stop by was C.B. He introduced himself to Zeke and his dad. Then he asked Rooster, "When will dinner be ready?"

"Whenever I call you ta eat, is when!" Rooster hollered, then chuckled. Pretty soon, he had a campfire going and was making coffee, beans, steaks, and biscuits.

C.B. was the first to come in when Rooster rang the dinner bell. Then they heard Rabbit riding in fast, hooting and hollering. He shook Jeff's hand, then grabbed Zeke and swung him around.

"Man! They sure are making cowboys smaller these days!" he said and laughed.

Boots rode in slowly. He tied up his horse and washed up at the back of the wagon. He was a well-worn cowboy. His scars seemed to match his clothes, which were all torn and scratched.

Zeke watched him uncertainly. Then Boots smiled and said, "Zeke, glad to meet ya! Good help is hard to find these days."

As they ate watching the sun set, Zeke asked, "Where is Coop?"

Rabbit laughed and pointed to a hilltop. "Still out there... as usual," he said.

After supper, they listened to Boots tell stories about stray cattle, rattlesnakes, blizzards, and the like. When Coop finally rode in to camp, Zeke watched him unsaddle and wipe down his horse. When he slowly settled in the corner with his plate, Boots introduced him to everyone.

Jeff could tell his son was not quite ready to ask any questions. So they just sat and laughed at the stories. Soon, Rooster dragged out the bedrolls, and they all climbed in and settled down.

They all said good night, and Boots added, "Good night, Zeke. I'm glad you're here. I need the help."

After a few minutes, Coop softly said, "Good night, Mr. Buffington. Good night, Zeke. May God bless."

Zeke had just about dozed off when he heard Coop's words. His eyes opened wide and he looked over at his dad. Then he slowly drifted off to sleep.

Chapter 12

They woke up to the rich smell of coffee and bacon, and the sounds of song birds. They also heard Rooster rattling pots and pans, and talking to himself.

Zeke's dad slowly rolled out of the sleeping bag to stretch his back. Zeke popped out and walked over to Rooster to ask for a cup of coffee.

"You'uns drink coffee?" Rooster asked. "That'll stunt your growin'," he said, laughing. Then he poured a cup for Zeke.

Dressed and ready for work, C.B., Boots, and Rabbit came up, leading their horses. C.B. asked if breakfast was ready yet.

Rabbit grabbed Zeke and swung him around, spilling his coffee. All the while, Boots was fussing at him to put the boy down. "It's too early for horse play!" he said.

Zeke asked, "Where's Coop?" as Rooster refilled his coffee cup.

"He'll be along in a minute," said Rooster. "Y'all come git your plate and eats." They lined up at the back of the chuck wagon, and Rooster filled their plate with biscuits, bacon, and gravy.

As they sat down to eat, Coop came up, and Rooster handed him his plate. "How was your quiet time?" asked Rabbit, in a not very nice way.

"Peaceful," Coop said and smiled. "You should get up early and come with me some morning."

"No way! I need my beauty sleep," Rabbit said, laughing.

"Wouldn't be quiet for you if he did come," said Boots.

After breakfast, the men packed the extra biscuits and bacon into their saddle bags. Rooster began cleaning up and packing the wagon to head back. Zeke and his dad helped some, but mostly stood out of his way. They watched as Rooster put pots, pans, and supplies into cubby holes, and tied things down all over the wagon.

As the cowboys mounted up to head out, Boots rode over. He asked Zeke and his dad if they would be coming back later. But before they could answer, Scooter rode up. He was leading Blaze and another horse, and both horses wore a saddle.

Scooter said, "You had a call from your office last night, Mr. Buffington. They wanted to know if you could call back today. I thought you might like riding a horse back to the ranch, instead of sitting in the chuck wagon."

"Thank you," Zeke's dad said. "The wagon did give me a back ache."

"Dad, would it be okay if I stay and watch the cowboys for a while?" Zeke asked.

"Well, I don't know. They have real work to do, and you might be in the way. And you'd have to be on a horse a good part of the day."

"He's more than welcome to stay," replied Boots. "We'll teach him the ropes, and make a real cowboy out of him."

Coop pointed to Blaze. "He'll have the best horse on the ranch, Mr. Buffington. And we'll look after him."

"Then it's okay with me," Zeke's dad said.

Scooter helped Zeke up onto Blaze, then gave him a few pointers. Within a few minutes, everyone agreed that Zeke looked like he was born to ride a horse.

Chapter 13

Zeke spent most of the morning following behind Boots. He watched the cowboys stop to fix fences as they slowly herded the cows along.

While they rode, Boots told him how the Lazy Bar Z Ranch was a real working ranch. He said the cattle business was not going well, so the Parkers decided to add a dude ranch.

"Most folks like to hang out at the lake and go trail riding," he said. "Sometimes, they watch us work. But not too many want to stay overnight like you did, so that makes you kinda special. You aimin' to be a real cowboy?"

"No, I want to be a football player," Zeke said. "But I like watching cowboy movies. Dad says cowboys are real tough. I think he wanted to be one a long time ago."

Boots just laughed. "It is kinda hard work, but I think football players are pretty tough, too."

After a minute, Zeke added, "I came here to find out if

cowboys pray."

Boots stopped his horse and turned to look at Zeke. "Wow, that's a first!" he said. "I've had a bunch of questions from youngsters visiting the ranch. They ask how I catch a cow or saddle a horse. Some want to know if cows sleep at night. But nobody ever asked about praying before."

"Do you pray?" Zeke asked.

Boots took off his hat and wiped his brow. "I have prayed on occasion, I suppose. I mean I believe in God and all. But I'm not exactly what you'd call a praying man."

Zeke was a little disappointed, but it was almost the answer he expected. Boots put his hat on, and pointed over at Coop. "You might want to ride along with Coop for a while. He knows more about stuff like that. He doesn't talk much, though. He likes to be alone in what he calls his quiet time."

Zeke joined Coop and the two rode ahead of everyone. Every now and then, Coop would hop off and tug on a strand of barb wire to be sure it was tight enough. Sometimes, he would take his fence pliers and pull one a little tighter. He even let Zeke drive a couple of nails into fence posts.

It seemed to Zeke that Coop really enjoyed his work. So he asked, "Have you always been a cowboy?" But Coop just looked off in the distance and didn't answer.

By late afternoon, Zeke's dad was still back at the ranch house, having a meeting over the phone with some people back at his office. Rooster had already headed back out to feed everybody. After thinking and praying about it, Zeke's dad decided it was okay to let his son spend the night out on the ranch without him.

As the day passed, the sky had filled with dark clouds. Toward the end of the afternoon, Rabbit galloped his horse over to Zeke and Coop. "You better get your quiet time in early," he said to Coop. "Looks like we have bad weather coming in. Boots told him to settle the herd down for the evening.

Rabbit nodded, then hollered, "Waaahooo! There comes Rooster! I'm starving!" With that, he went galloping off.

Coop just shook his head, "That cowboy is wild," he said to Zeke. "I hope he'll settle down one day, and learn some respect." He finished nailing a piece of barbed wire, then added, "You know, you *can* be a tough cowboy without being a mean one."

Chapter 14

The wind began kicking up, and dark clouds formed on the horizon. Coop and Zeke helped the others herd the cattle into a tighter group for the night.

Coop told Zeke how to ride around the cows that had not settled down. He taught Zeke how to have his horse Blaze, back up and how to cut side to side. This kept the cows from getting past him. As Zeke and Blaze worked the cows, the others yelled to Zeke, "Way to go, cowboy!" Every time they did, Zeke grinned from ear to ear.

When all of the cows were finally settled, everyone rode over to Rooster and the chuck wagon. The fire was going, and they could smell the steaks, beans, and biscuits cooking. Rooster had already put up tents, to keep them dry in case it rained.

Coop told Zeke, "Go and get ready to eat. I'm gonna ride over to that little ridge for a while."

"Are you going for your quiet time, Mr. Coop?" Zeke

asked. "Can I go with you?"

Coop turned to look at Zeke. Then he smiled and said, "It would be a pleasure to have you join me."

Coop and Zeke rode to the low ridge with a lone tree. They tied the horses to the tree and sat on the ground to watch the sun go down. It shot out orange and yellow rays from behind dark clouds. Coop said, "This sure is beautiful, isn't it? God creates beauty even in the middle of storms."

Zeke had been trying to decide how to ask Coop a special question. Now, he said, "My dad and I saw a rainbow a few weeks ago. That's what led us to take this trip."

"You don't say! That must have been some rainbow," Coop replied.

"Yeah, we were talking about how we should thank God for it. And I asked Dad about who prays. Then I asked if cowboys pray. Dad said we should talk to some real cowboys, and then I could find out for myself."

"Wow, that's pretty remarkable!" Coop said. "Why did you ask that?"

"I don't know. I guess, because cowboys are tough. I know some tough kids at school. They don't pray, and they make fun of me. So I figured if cowboys don't pray…" Zeke stopped, not sure what he was trying to say.

They sat in silence for a few minutes, watching lightning flash in the dark clouds. Then Coop said, "I come here every evening to sit by myself and look out at God's creation. I wonder why He created such a beautiful world for us. Even the storms are magnificent!

"I do pray, Zeke. I pray every day, thanking God for His beautiful creations. I pray for people all over the world. I pray for peace. And I pray that more people will come to know God through His Son, Jesus. I also pray for other cowboys, like Rabbit, who don't have a relationship with God."

A little puzzled, Zeke asked, "You pray for other cowboys that don't pray, even if they pick on you?"

"Absolutely! Being picked on doesn't bother a tough guy," Coop responded with a wink. "You asked if I had always been a cowboy. I grew up on a ranch and learned to rope and ride as a little boy. I worked with my uncle on his ranch until I was eighteen.

"My parents died when I was very young. After I graduated from high school, I joined the Navy, and moved away. I was part of an elite unit called the Navy Seals. Have you heard of them?"

"Yeah, I saw a movie about them. Those guys are super tough, too," Zeke said.

"Yeah, you could say that. I traveled all over the world, and saw a lot of beautiful places, and met a lot of wonderful people. I served with some of the bravest and toughest men and women I have ever known. Some of them died in battle.

"I came here after getting out of the Navy, to work on Mr. Parker's ranch. I think I will be a cowboy for the rest of my life." He turned to smile at Zeke and added. "I'll always be a praying cowboy, too!"

With that, Coop bowed his head, and began to pray. He thanked God for His majestic creation, the beautiful sunset, and the storms of life that strengthen us. He prayed for the people that are suffering and lost and the cowboys that don't know God. And he prayed for protection for the people and animals on the ranch.

Then he thanked God for the food that Rooster was preparing. And he closed by thanking God for Zeke, who was seeking wisdom and knowledge by asking if cowboys pray. He prayed that God would give Zeke the heart of a praying cowboy, the boldness to pray, and the toughness, and courage to love even those that may not care to pray.

Chapter 15

As they headed back to camp, Zeke was beaming. He had a real cowboy praying with him, one who asked God to give him the "heart of a cowboy, toughness and boldness." Wow!

The storm was getting closer. The wind was picking up, and a light rain had begun. When they arrived at camp, Rooster came over and handed Zeke a poncho and plate. "This'll keep ya dry," he said. "Hop inta that tent 'tween Boots and Coop. You not afeared to sleep in there, are ya?"

"No, sir, Mr. Rooster. I'll be fine," Zeke said, still beaming.

Luckily, the storm missed the camp. They heard a lot of rumbling and saw flashes of lightning, but there was very little rain.

When Zeke woke up the next morning, Rooster was preparing breakfast, and Boots was barking orders. Apparently, the thunder and lightning had scared a bunch of the cows off. So Boots told C.B. and Rabbit to find out which way they went. Rabbit was mumbling and grumbling, but he left to ride toward the stream, as C.B. went in the other direction, up over the ridge.

Coop volunteered to take the trail they had come down the day before, and asked if Zeke wanted to go with him. They mounted up quickly and took off. Within a few minutes, they found some of the cows standing under a clump of trees. After rounding them up, Coop and Zeke started moving the cows back toward camp. Zeke quickly got the hang of herding, and had lots of fun waving the rope and yelling, "Move 'em out!"

Back at camp, they learned C.B. had found a couple of the cows and moved them into the rest of the herd. Boots said he found about five up ahead near the trail. He decided to leave them, since the herd would be driven that way shortly. Rooster handed the crew their breakfast plates, and they sat by the fire to eat.

By the time they finished breakfast, Rabbit still wasn't back. Rooster packed the wagon while the team got the herd ready to move.

Boots told Coop, "You better go find Rabbit. He's probably asleep under a tree, still mad I sent him out before breakfast."

Coop said, "Sure thing. Can Zeke come along?"

"Sure," said Boots. "But hurry back. I need Zeke more than I need Rabbit!"

Chapter 16

Zeke and Coop took off and rode over the ridge. Coop showed Zeke how to follow the tracks that Rabbit's horse made in the soft dirt. They rode toward the stream and were surprised to see it had swollen into a raging river. It hadn't rained much at their camp, but it had rained a lot upland. And that water was finding its way into the stream, creating a flash flood.

The horse tracks they were following went in both directions. Coop studied them for a minute then made a decision. "Let's go this way," he said to Zeke, and pointed downstream.

As they rode slowly along the stream bank, Coop told Zeke to move Blaze away from the edge of the fast-moving water. Suddenly, they heard someone calling in the distance. The sound was hard to hear over the noise of the stream, but a little further along, they saw Rabbit. He was hanging on to a small tree out in the stream. The rushing water was bubbling over him, and he was having trouble hanging on.

"Hold on!" yelled Coop. "Don't let go!"

Coop jumped off his horse and pulled off his gun belt, hat, and boots. He said, "Zeke, I need your help. We've got to save Rabbit. You can do this." Then he took the rope off Zeke's saddle, tied a knot over the saddle horn, and tied the other end around his own waist.

"I'm going to swim to where Rabbit is," he told Zeke. "Once I get my arms and legs around him, I'll nod my head. When I do that, you get Blaze to back up as fast as you can, okay? Remember how we did that yesterday?" "Yes, sir. I point my toes forward, then hold my hands down low and pull back on the reins."

"Good! Back Blaze up over there," Coop said, pointing to a flat area. "That will give Blaze good footing."

Zeke did exactly as Coop said. "That was good," Coop told him. "Now, one last thing. Once Blaze is backing up as fast as he can, don't stop until you see Rabbit and me on the bank. We'll go under the water and you won't see us for a few minutes, but don't be afraid. Just keep backing up, okay?"

Zeke was suddenly scared, but he managed to stutter, "Yes, sir."

Coop looked him in the eye and said, "That's the way to cowboy up! Let's do it!"

Coop pulled the rope out to make sure it wouldn't get tangled. Then he glanced toward heaven, turned around and ran toward the water. At the edge, he dove as far as he could into the water.

He hit the water and paddled hard toward the tree where Rabbit was hanging on. Zeke watched carefully as Coop cut through the water, grabbed Rabbit and unbuckled Rabbit's gun belt that was caught on the tree. Then Coop looked at Zeke and nodded his head.

Right away, Zeke backed Blaze up. Suddenly, Rabbit and Coop went under the water. Zeke cried and shook, but he kept backing Blaze up further and further. Finally, the rope pulled Rabbit and Coop up on the bank. Coop let go of Rabbit and waved for Zeke to stop.

Zeke stopped Blaze, then jumped down and ran over to Coop, who was out of breath. Rabbit was choking and gasping for air. Coop rolled him over, and began pumping the water out by pushing down on his back. As he worked, Coop prayed, "Father God, please let him live. Father God, please let him live. Father God, please let him live." After a minute, water spewed out of Rabbit's mouth. Then he coughed and began breathing on his own.

It was several long minutes before Coop could get back to his feet. Then he knelt back down beside Rabbit, who caught his breath enough to sit up. Zeke fell to his knees as well. He was trembling and tears streamed down his face. But he was smiling, and happy that everyone was okay.

Coop said, "Rabbit, you sure are one lucky outlaw to have a cowboy like Zeke riding along. He just saved your life."

Rabbit started shaking, and his eyes filled with tears. He looked at Zeke and said in a trembling voice, "Thank you! I was praying that God would rescue me. I wasn't sure if there really was a God or not. But, now I *know* there is! Thank you!"

Chapter 17

The first day of school was like all the others. Zeke was glad to see all of his old friends, meet his new teachers, and explore the new campus.

Standing in line for lunch, Zeke spotted Bobby in the cafeteria. Bobby was cutting in line and picking on one of the smaller kids. Zeke got his tray, filled his plate, and found a place to sit. He was quietly bowing his head to say grace when someone bumped his arm and plopped down beside him.

"Hey, Zeke," Bobby said in a loud voice. "What are you up to? Are you praying that the cafeteria food won't kill you? Ha! Ha!"

Zeke finished praying and looked up at Bobby. Then, remembering the words of his friend Coop, he said with a smile, "No, Bobby…I was praying for you."

Dear Reader,

I hope you enjoyed reading *Daddy, Do Cowboys Pray*. I

pray you are inspired to be courageous and bold about praying. I pray you will continue to grow your relationship with God.

If you are just learning to pray, do so boldly, walk in confidence that God is with you and desires to use you.

As you grow, you will become stronger in prayer and courageous in the face of difficulty.

If you have not yet accepted Jesus Christ as your Lord and Savior, below are some verses you need to understand, followed by the *most* important prayer you can ever pray.

They are not magic words, but real words that must be felt and meant as you pray.

John 3:16

For God so loved the world that He gave His one and only Son, that whoever believes in Him shall not perish but have eternal life.

Romans 3:23

For all have sinned and fall short of the glory of God.

Romans 6:23

For the wages of sin is death, but the gift of God is eternal life in Christ Jesus our Lord.

Romans 5:8

But God demonstrates His own love for us in this: While we were still sinners, Christ died for us.

Romans 10:13

for, "Everyone who calls on the name of the Lord will be saved."

Romans 10:9,10

If you declare with your mouth, "Jesus is Lord," and believe in your heart that God raised him from the dead, you will be saved.

When Jesus died on the cross He paid our price for sin. He freed us out of slavery to sin and death! The only condition is that we must believe in Him and what He has done for us. We have to understand that we are now joined with Him, and that He is our life. He did all this because He loved us and gave Himself for us!

If you feel that God is knocking on your heart's door, ask Him to come into your heart by praying the following:

"Dear God, I know that I have broken your laws. My sins are what keeps me from You. I am truly sorry, and now I want to turn away from my past life. Please forgive me. I believe that Your Son, Jesus Christ, died for my sins, was raised from the dead, is alive, and hears my prayers. I invite Jesus to come into my life, to live in my heart from this day forward. Please send Your Holy Spirit to help me obey You, and to do Your will for the rest of my life. In Jesus' name I pray, Amen."

Welcome to God's Kingdom, I pray you will continue to be strong in your faith, study your Bible and pray for those who do not yet know God!

Now go and be courageous!

Need additional copies?

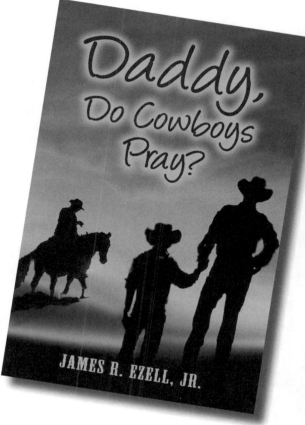

To order more copies of

Daddy, Do Cowboys Pray?

contact NewBookPublishing.com

☐   Order online at

NewBookPublishing.com/Bookstore

☐   Call 877-311-5100 or

☐   Email Info@NewBookPublishing.com

 **Reliance Media**